LITTLE

DOLPHiN

RESCUE

STRIPES PUBLISHING LIMITED
An imprint of the Little Tiger Group
1 Coda Studios, 189 Munster Road, London SW6 6AW

A paperback original
First published in Great Britain in 2019

Text copyright © Rachel Delahaye, 2019
Inside illustrations copyright © Artful Doodlers, 2019
Cover illustration copyright © Suzie Mason, 2019

ISBN: 978-1-78895-073-2

A CIP catalogue record for this book is available from the British Library.

Printed and bound in the UK.

2 4 6 8 10 9 7 5 3 1

LITTLE
DOLPHIN
RESCUE

Rachel Delahaye

Stripes

For Grace, who can't choose a favourite animal
but thinks it might be a dolphin
– Rachel

CONTENTS

Splash!

"Look! There's a sea monster in the swimming pool," said Ella.

"Nice try," laughed Fliss. "But I don't believe you."

"You never fall for my pranks any more," moaned Ella.

Fliss and Ella were sitting on the edge of the pool, waiting for their swimming lesson. They dangled their legs in the water, swishing them backwards and forwards.

"Do you see that bug?" Ella said suddenly. "Over there. It's drowning!"

"There's no bug." Fliss shook her head.

"This time I mean it, Fliss! There is, honestly."

Fliss sighed. Ella knew her so well – she knew that Fliss would have to look, just in case it was true. Because if there was a bug and she let it drown, she would be upset. Fliss loved all animals and wanted to be a vet when she grew up.

"Where is it, then?" Fliss leaned forwards. "Show me."

Ella put her hand in the pool but instead of pointing out the beetle, she cupped up some water and threw it in Fliss's face.

"Got you!" she shouted happily.

Fliss shrieked. She was about to splash Ella back when their teacher blew his whistle. It was time for their lesson to begin. "I'll get you later!" she said with a giggle.

The girls lined up by the pool with the rest of the swimming class – including

their friends Maya, Karl, Huey and
Kevin – and Mr Luck clapped his hands
for attention. "Hello, everyone," he said.

"Hello, Mr Luck!" The greeting
echoed around the poolroom.

"I'm sorry you haven't had a lesson
for three weeks. It took longer than
we thought to redecorate! But what do
you think of the newly painted leisure
centre?"

"That's awesome!" said Maya,
pointing to a beach scene painted on the
walls.

"Just wait until you see what's
underwater at the deep end," Mr
Luck said with a wink. "Now, I have
an announcement. We are starting an
under-twelves swimming team and we
need a name. Give me your best ideas

at the end of the lesson and I'll choose a winner."

"What do we win?" asked Maya.

"Is it a tropical island holiday?" Ella squeezed Fliss's arm and jumped up and down.

Mr Luck laughed. "You'll have to wait and see!"

"Definitely a tropical holiday," Ella whispered in Fliss's ear.

"As a special treat, it's a free-play lesson today. Help yourselves to inflatables but don't forget to go for a swim in the deep end. I think you're going to like what you see!"

The children jumped into the pool. By the time Fliss had adjusted the straps on her goggles, the whole of the shallow end was churned up with splashing. Ella had found a giant donut and was floating in the middle of the pool, as Karl and his friends tried to flip her over.

"Help me, Fliss!" Ella called, kicking water in their faces.

Fliss was tempted to join in with Karl to pay Ella back for her trick, but she wanted to check out Mr Luck's underwater surprise while the deep end was quiet.

Fliss was nervous about being out of her depth, so she stayed close to the side of the pool where she could grip the edge if she needed to. When her feet could no longer touch the bottom, she put her face in the water…

Wow!

The walls of the deep end were painted to look like a tropical reef.

Splash!

There was coral, seaweed and marine life like fish, octopuses, starfish and sharks. And it wasn't cartoony, like a lot of murals. In fact, with all the detail, it was easy to imagine that a real-life reef shark might suddenly appear...

Just then, a dark shape passed beneath her. Fliss caught her breath and grabbed the edge of the pool. But when she looked down, she saw it wasn't a sea monster – it was Huey! What was he doing?

Huey was gliding along the bottom of the pool with his arms by his side and his legs together. He kicked them at the same time, as if he were flipping a tail! He looked very much at home against the backdrop of the reef. Fliss kept holding the edge of the pool and waited for him to come up for air.

"Hey, Huey, can you teach me how to do that swimming stroke?"

"The dolphin-kick? Sure, it's easy! Just keep your arms by your sides and your legs together. Roll your body from head to toe, and kick your feet together last. Oh, and don't forget to hold your breath!"

Huey disappeared back down to the bottom of the pool and Fliss took a moment to demist her goggles and think. The water was deep and that scared her, but if she stayed close to the side of the pool she'd be OK. She let herself sink a little below the surface and tried Huey's dolphin-kick. But although she thought she had followed Huey's instructions, it was more of a going-nowhere thrash than an elegant dolphin swim!

"What am I doing wrong?" she asked when Huey came up again.

"It works better if you go deeper." Fliss look worried so Huey added, "Follow me and you'll be fine. One, two, three…"

They both took a deep breath and swam down, using their arms to go lower and lower. Once they were at the bottom of the pool, Huey began to roll

his body, propelling himself through
the water with a final kick. Fliss soon
got the hang of it too. Roll and kick,
roll and kick! She even started to feel at
home in the water, as if she was a sea
creature herself.

Splash!

Fliss reached the back wall of the pool and came up for air, grinning. She had swum underwater for at least five metres without panicking!

Huey popped up next to her. "You're a natural," he said.

"I am?" said Fliss, unable to hide her pride.

"Yep. A pod of dolphins would be happy to hang out with you!"

"Fliss!" shrieked Ella as Karl spun the donut round and round. "Come and get dizzy! It's fuuuuuun!"

Not as fun as swimming like a dolphin, Fliss thought. She laughed at Ella then ducked back underwater. With her feet flat against the wall she pushed herself back down into the deep and Huey followed.

Rays from the ceiling lights pierced the water and sent reflections rippling across the mural. Fliss imagined that it was all real – the eel in the coral, the starfish on the rock, the shoal of blue and yellow fish. The more she thought, the clearer the pictures seemed and the brighter they became. And then Fliss stopped kicking. Was that shoal of fish actually moving? *Of course not*, she thought. It was just a trick of the light.

Then something swam alongside her. Huey? It glided by her with a flap of its enormous wings.

No, it wasn't Huey.

Washed Up in Paradise

There was a manta ray in the swimming pool! Fliss had to tell someone immediately. Surely, *that* wasn't part of Mr Luck's underwater surprise?

She put her feet on the bottom and realized she could stand up – she was no longer out of her depth. Had she swum all the way to the shallow end? Why was there sand beneath her feet? Fliss was confused, especially as her goggles had misted up and she

13

couldn't see a thing.

"Mr Luck?" she called, taking off her goggles and rubbing her eyes. As she said his name, she noticed something strange. Just a minute ago, the pool had sounded like a baboon party, and now it was silent. Had everyone gone?

When she could finally see, Fliss couldn't believe her eyes. Yes, everyone *had* gone. Huey, Ella, Karl, Mr Luck – the whole class! Even the pool had gone. Fliss was now standing up to her waist in turquoise seawater, by a white sandy beach.

"A tropical island?" Fliss laughed. It was like a picture postcard, a place you only saw in expensive holiday brochures… But what was she doing here? And how was she going to get back? Mr Luck always did a head count at the end of the lesson and he would be worried if she was missing.

Fliss knelt down so she was completely underwater. There was nothing but crystal-clear water and shoals of fish in all different shapes and colours and patterns! Maybe she could spend a little more time here before trying to find her way back home…

The sun sparkles danced on the water and Fliss shielded her eyes so she could look around. There was no one on the beach but there was a small building not far along. The owner would be able to tell her where she was.

Fliss watched the pretty fish dart away for safety as she waded through the water. But they weren't the only pretty things at her feet. Scattered across the seabed were shells. They were so shiny and beautiful they looked like jewels. Fliss wanted to run her hands through them, like a pirate enjoying her treasure! As she reached down, her hand brushed against a large brown disc. It floated upwards and then sank back down, landing on its other side.

The shell was as big as her hand and

looked like mother-of-pearl – silvery, with dashes of purple, green and blue. The colours swirled together like a liquid rainbow. It was mesmerizing. As she walked towards the beach, she gazed at the seashell in her hand.

OUCH!

Fliss's foot began to sting and throb. She must have cut it on something! Clutching her beautiful shell, she hobbled along the beach to the building she had seen, hoping there would be someone there who could help.

Izad's Fruit Shack was a tiny juice bar. It had a couple of tables and chairs on the sand and a hatch in the wall. Fliss hopped forwards and peered through the hatch.

"Hello? Is anyone there?"

A tall man rose from behind the counter with a sleepy smile. He wore a little straw hat and round his neck hung lots and lots of necklaces, some plain, some with painted beads.

"Izad at your service. Mango juice, coconut water, what do you fancy?"

"Hello, Izad, my name's Fliss. I cut my foot in the sea and I was hoping you could help me?"

Izad looked concerned. "Take a seat and I'll be right there."

Fliss sat and Izad appeared with a medical bag and a bottle of water, which he poured over the cut to clean out the sand.

"Looks like a shell cut," he tutted. "Broken shells can be very nasty. But this isn't too deep." Fliss winced as Izad

18

dabbed on some antiseptic. Then he took out a plaster and popped it on top. "You'll be fine in no time," he said with a huge smile.

"Thank you!" said Fliss, and then she remembered the beautiful shell. "Oh, and could you tell me what sort of shell this is?" she asked, showing him her find.

"That's an abalone."

"*Ah-bah-lone-ee.*" Fliss sounded it out.

"You're not going to keep it, are you?"
Izad asked. Fliss's face must have fallen
because he wagged his finger. "What
belongs to the sea must be returned to
the sea. But you can look after it while
you're here. Have this."

Izad took off one of his plain string
necklaces. He threaded it through a
hole in the shell and then tied it around
Fliss's neck.

"You look like a proper tropical island
girl now."

"Thank you, Izad," said Fliss. "I
promise I'll give it back to the sea when
I leave."

"Thank *you*, Fliss." Izad smiled.
"Here on Payocos we look after our

environment.
We live as part
of the island.
We don't own it."

"I think your
island is the most
beautiful place
I've ever seen!"

"You haven't seen half of it yet!"
said Izad. He pointed out to sea.
"Payocos is surrounded by a ring of
shallow coral reef. It goes all the way
from here to Coral Point, over in the
distance. We call it the Blue Halo.
Explore it and you'll see why we are so
keen to protect it. Now, wait here."

Izad disappeared and returned a
minute later with a yellow drink, a
snorkelling mask and two small socks.

"Coconut and pineapple," he said as he handed her the drink. "A taste of Payocos just for you."

Fliss took a sip and sighed. It was totally yummy!

"And here is a mask so you can see the reef better."

"Thank you! Those are funny flippers," said Fliss, pointing at the socks.

"Not flippers. Flippers damage coral. These are reef slippers," Izad replied.

"Do they protect the coral from human germs?" asked Fliss.

Izad tipped back his head and let out a deep laugh that made Fliss want to laugh too. "No. They're to stop your plaster from falling off!"

The Underwater Playground

Fliss waded into the water with her new slippers and mask and looked back at Izad. He was standing on the beach with his hands on his hips and a big friendly smile.

"You're going to love it!" he said, full of pride. "Payocos is very special. You'll see."

"Is it safe to swim?" asked Fliss. She was worried that if she got out of her depth there would be nothing to hang on to. She wasn't in a pool now.

"Inside the ring of coral the water never gets too deep, so it's safe to swim there. On the other side of the reef – outside the Blue Halo where the water gets dark – that's deep. It's not dangerous, but if you're nervous you should stay inside the reef."

Fliss stepped further into the crystal waters, feeling reassured by Izad's answer.

"Watch out for lions, zebras and parrots!" Izad shouted.

What? Fliss spun round.

Izad took one look at her face and burst out laughing. "They're types of fish!" he hooted, slapping his thigh. Then he wandered back to his juice bar and Fliss could still hear him laughing as she swam out into the Blue Halo.

Wearing Izad's mask, Fliss put her head underwater. Wow! She could see everything so clearly – even groups of playful fish much further out. Below her, hermit crabs scuttled across the sandy seabed, dragging their brightly coloured houses behind them.

The further Fliss went out, the more the underwater landscape changed. There were rocks and different types of coral – some spread out like fans and others clustered together like cauliflowers. Bigger fish appeared with pouty lips and large eyes. Some had funny markings and Fliss laughed when she saw a group that looked as if they had angry eyebrows.

It was an underwater paradise, and this was only a small piece of it. The Blue Halo reef was vast. Fliss continued swimming away from the island, spotting eels snooping in the rocks and starfish the size of dinner plates. She even saw a puffer fish that had blown up like a balloon and was bobbing about like a spiky melon.

Just as Izad said – the reef was

shallow and safe. Even if Fliss had
a reason to be nervous, she was too
distracted to worry. The colours and
the creatures were breathtaking. Even
the sounds were amazing – the gentle
lapping of the water, the crackling as
fish sucked up and spat out stones, the
popping of air bubbles coming from
holes in the rocks. And the clicking.

What *was* the clicking?

The water was getting a little deeper now and the walls of coral were thicker, brighter and teeming with life. The funny clicking noise was getting louder. Fliss swam down a channel between the coral, just as something large was swimming up it. The thing was heading right towards her...

A shark? Fliss's breath caught in her throat. There was nowhere to go, nothing to do except keep her face in the water so she could see what was coming. But then she recognized the swimming stroke... Roll and kick, roll and kick. A dolphin!

It was only a little one – no bigger than a dog – with pretty stripes of black, grey and white along the length of its body. When the dolphin got closer, Fliss reached out to touch it but it dodged her hand, shot past her and vanished into the coral. It emerged from another clump of coral and made its way towards her again. Then it rushed past her, vanished and reappeared, over and over, clicking and squealing all the time. It reminded Fliss of an excited child and, judging by the size of it, it had to be a baby.

When the dolphin swam past her
on its side, revealing the smile-shaped
curve of its mouth, Fliss clapped. At
the sound, the dolphin slowed down. It
swam up to her. It looked curious. Fliss
clapped her hands again and the dolphin
bobbed its head.

You like that, do you? Fliss thought.
Well, how about if I sing?

Fliss hummed a tune. It sounded
funny underwater but the dolphin
seemed to like it. Now it came so
close that Fliss could have touched it
if she wanted to, but she didn't.
Instead she made more sounds and
the dolphin began to inspect her – it
looked right into her mask! Then a
sudden noise caused it to back away.
Fliss heard it too. A chorus of whistles,

so high-pitched they almost hurt her ears. The dolphin nodded. Then it was gone, 'dolphin-kicking' back down the watery channel and out of sight.

Fliss raised her head above the water. She was close to the outside edge of the Blue Halo. Over the next boundary of pale coral was the dark blue sea. And bursting out of it, spinning once, twice, three times before crashing back down, was the little dolphin. It did it again – spinning as if it was in a gymnastics show, falling with a splash back into the water.

It was putting on a display for her! As it leaped high once again, Fliss spotted a single groove on the dolphin's underside. She knew, from her *World of Dolphins* book, that females had two

slits, side by side. This was definitely a
boy.

"Well done, Spinner!" she called. The
name came to her instantly. Yes, Spinner
was the perfect name for the little
dolphin.

Spinner then performed a single jump,
a perfect arc. The sea spray caught the
sun and a colourful rainbow curved
above her head.

"You're a very special dolphin, aren't you, Spinner?" Fliss said.

But Spinner was gone.

The Catch

Fliss swam along the edge of the reef, looking for a gap into the deep sea. Spinner must have made it through somewhere! But all she could see was a thick boundary of coral and thousands of dazzling fish.

She found a rocky boulder and climbed on to it carefully, so as not to crush the sea snails that clung to it. It was the perfect lookout because when she stood up – wow! – she felt as if she was standing on the water, right in the middle of the ocean. On one side was the turquoise water full of bright fish and coral, and on the other, the dark blue sea. What that was full of, she didn't know – she was only interested in spotting Spinner.

Spinner didn't appear, but Fliss did see a group of boats heading her way. As they got closer, Fliss could see that the boats were named – *Fortune*, *Amour* and *Belle*. They towed small brightly coloured wooden boats behind them, like a shoal of tropical fish.

Fliss wondered if, like Spinner, they knew about a secret gap to get through the Blue Halo. But the boats slowed down before they reached the reef, dropped their anchors and groups of men and women appeared on their decks.

"Hi!" A woman dressed in shorts and a vest top waved at Fliss.

"Hello!" Fliss waved back. "What are you doing?"

"Do you want to come and see?"

Fliss hesitated. It was only a short swim over to the boats, but it would mean crossing the deep blue water.

"I'll swim with you, if you like," the woman said. "I could do with cooling off. I'm Sandy, by the way!"

Then – splash! – she jumped overboard and swam towards Fliss. She bobbed in the dark water between the boats and the reef. With an adult around, Fliss felt more confident and she jumped right in.

The Catch

Fliss swam alongside Sandy. She couldn't believe it! She was swimming in deep water! Just a few more strokes and she was at the boat called *Belle*. She climbed the ladder and everyone on board gave her a welcome cheer. Along with all the people on the deck there was a huge net, wriggling with fish.

"Our haul for the market!" Sandy explained, pointing to the net.

"But why have you stopped here?" Fliss asked. "Why don't you take the boats to the shore?"

"The reef is too shallow and we don't want to damage the coral. We'll sort through the fish here on board and take our catch to the island on the *pirogues*." She pointed to the pretty wooden boats tied up behind.

"Can I help you sort the fish?"

"Absolutely!" Sandy beamed. "But it's not just fish you have to handle. A whole range of creatures get caught in our nets. This morning, a huge sea turtle got trapped."

"Is it still here?" asked Fliss, peering into the net.

"No, we jumped in and cut it free. We lost a piece of the net, though – we're alerting all of Payocos's boats to look out for it. We don't want it hurting the wildlife. But usually we pull up squid, octopuses and eels. Do you think you'll be OK handling them?"

"I'm not sure," Fliss said, honestly. "But when I grow up I want to be a vet, so it's good experience."

Sandy gave a thumbs up. "That's a great attitude. I think you have exactly what it takes to be a vet. Bravery!"

One of Sandy's fishing crew unhooked a piece of the net and it slid open, releasing the catch. Fish of all sizes flipped and flapped on the deck and octopuses oozed over the top of them, looking for an escape. Shark-like creatures jerked angrily from side to side.

"Sharks!" Fliss said, alarmed.

"Yes, sharks! Tourists always worry about sharks," Sandy laughed. "Do you know, we've never had a shark attack in Payocos? There are lots of shark species out there," she said, pointing out to sea, "but they've never bothered us. If a shark ever does come near, just bop it on the nose."

Fliss smiled with relief. It was good to know that sharks weren't a problem.

"Shall I start by picking up the octopuses?"

"They can find their own way back to the sea – they slither overboard!" said Sandy. "And actually, octopuses have a sharp beak and can give you a nasty bite. It's better if you start by throwing back the little fish and rays. The baby sharks too. Hold them up by the tail and tummy and give them a good heave overboard."

Before she could talk herself out it, Fliss reached into the pile of slithering fish. As her hand touched the cold slime, she reminded herself that one day she might have to help a calf being born or perform an operation on a poorly pet.

Getting gooey was good practice!

Fliss quickly became used to the slime and worked happily alongside her new friends who sang enchanting songs about the sea. When the tiddlers and unwanted sea creatures had been thrown back, they passed buckets of good-sized fish to people on the *pirogues,* to be paddled across the shallow water to Payocos.

"You did a great job, Fliss," Sandy said. "Do you want a lift to shore?"

"I think I'd like to spend more time on the reef," Fliss said. The hard work had made her hot and sweaty, and the bright blue water looked inviting.

"I can swim you back if you like?" Sandy smiled.

Fliss looked at the dark water. She

could do it now. It wasn't about ability, it was about bravery. Just like sticking her hand in with the slimy fish, she had to get on with it.

"Thanks, Sandy, but I think I can manage on my own," said Fliss, before leaping overboard and into the sea.

In a few short strokes, Fliss made it back to the reef. She watched as her fishing friends abandoned the *Belle*, the *Amour* and the *Fortune*, and set off on the pretty *pirogues* with their fresh catch.

Fliss put on her mask and immersed herself once more in the beautiful underwater world. It was a world she could never get bored of. But as she swam through the channels of coral, the thought returned – *why was she there?*

The Big Blue

"Why am I here?" Fliss asked aloud, hoping the reef would give her a sign. A sunken treasure chest jutting out of the sand or a message in a bottle would be useful. But there was only the continuous bustling life of the rainbow reef.

Fliss decided there was no point in worrying about it. And just in case she suddenly found herself back in the pool being splashed by Karl and Ella, she was determined to make the most of

her extraordinary visit to Payocos. She
paid attention to everything around her.
Watching animals go about their lives
was her favourite hobby.

Large crabs fed themselves busily,
shovelling bits and pieces from the seabed
into their mouths. Blue-and-yellow sea
slugs with funny horns and rippling skirts
slid over rocks. Sea anemones waved with
long tentacles that looked like Play-Doh.
All around, the water fizzed and
crackled with activity – the
sound of endless air
bubbles and a
million
creatures
pecking at
particles on
the reef.

And then she heard a squeal. Was it air escaping from a giant clam? Or the pressure of the water on the coral and sponges?

There was another one. It was high-pitched – a sound that wasn't in harmony with the reef. Over and over again it came. It sounded urgent. A cry for help. Then she heard the clicking – clicking and squealing, clicking and squealing – and Fliss knew. It was a dolphin in trouble.

Perhaps a dolphin had entered the reef and was stuck in the shallows. Fliss swam through the channels of the reef, searching for the lost dolphin, trying to follow its cries. They were so desperate and Fliss felt helpless. How was she going to find it? Not by swimming

round and round in circles. She needed
a better viewpoint so she could see a
large shape quickly and easily, just as
she'd seen Huey gliding below her at
the bottom of the pool. Of course! She
needed to look down!

Fliss found a large rock to stand on. It
raised her above the reef and she looked
out over the water, but the only dark
shapes she could see were clumps of coral.

Maybe the sound hadn't come from the
reef at all.

Fliss looked behind her at the deep sea.
Belle, *Amour* and *Fortune* were still there,
anchored until the next fishing trip. They
were only a few metres from the edge of
the reef. Not even as far as a length of
the swimming pool. She could swim that
easily. She already had! She could look

through her mask on the short journey across to see if a dolphin was there. She just had to be brave.

"Remember the vet's oath," Fliss reminded herself. "I must do everything in my power to help animals in need." She took another look at the deep water. "I can do it, I can do it, I can do it!"

And before she could change her mind, she leaped in.

The moment her head went under she heard the call. It was louder than before. The clicks were like bursting popcorn kernels, the squeals were sharp as knives. Fliss headed towards the boats, searching the waters as she swam.

Behind her, she saw the pale wall of the coral reef, bright with fish, before the seabed dipped down into unknown depths. Looking forwards, there was just the odd jellyfish bobbing along, or a slow-trailing shoal of fish. Apart from that, there was nothing. Nothing *she* could see, anyway. But that didn't mean there was nothing there in the great big blue…

Panic caught up with her bravery and Fliss's heart began thumping in her chest. The undersides of the boats ahead of her looked like floating icebergs and she swam towards them as fast as she could.

Then something touched her feet. Fliss squealed, drawing her legs up to her chest, and looked down, fearing jellyfish or something worse. It was bubbles. A stream of large bubbles was rising from the deep. Totally spooked, Fliss swam quickly to the boat. Once she was safely on the ladder, she caught her breath and began to think about the bubbles. Small bubbles escaped from plants and rocks all the time, but these were big. Something big was down there. Something that needed air. Sharks didn't need air. In fact, she'd read in *Nature Magazine* that they were scared by bubbles. But dolphins...

Fliss let go of the ladder. Leaving her fear at the surface, she swam as fast as she could, heading down into the depths, following the column of bubbles. Then she saw it. A little dolphin, twisting and turning, its flippers caught in a torn piece of orange net. The piece the fishing boat had lost!

The dolphin had black, grey and white markings and was small. As she swam closer, the dolphin saw her. It stopped twisting and nodded – its whole body bowing to her – and then it started to struggle again, bubbles escaping from the blowhole on top of its head as it struggled.

"Oh, Spinner!" Fliss's words came out in a strange squeak of her own. She put her face close to the little dolphin and stroked his nose.

I'm going up for air but I'll be back. I won't leave you, Spinner. I promise.

Fliss hoped he would understand. She kicked as hard as she could back to the surface and took a huge gulp of air. That's when she noticed a group of dorsal fins cutting through the water. They were moving fast and heading in her direction. Then they dipped under the water and vanished, and Fliss felt herself turn cold with fear.

6

Distress!

Fliss ducked her head underwater. Dolphins!

She wanted to cry with relief, although she still felt nervous. A huge pod of dolphins was an intimidating sight. But they weren't interested in her – they were heading towards Spinner. They must be Spinner's family. They'd know what to do!

Fliss didn't want to miss a minute. She took another deep breath and went down, hoping they wouldn't see her as a threat. She had to see Spinner released from his fishing-net prison. She wanted to see him spin in the air again, happy and free.

The big dolphins circled the baby one. Some nudged his body, others pushed at the net wrapped round his flippers. But the net was wound so many times and so tightly, it wouldn't move. There were panicked squeals and Fliss could sense the despair of the pod. And poor Spinner … he was running out of air.

"Spinner!" Fliss called underwater.

He saw her and lifted his head.

"I'm here! I'm not going to leave you."

The pod of dolphins stopped what

they were doing and turned to look at her. There in the deep blue water, Fliss wondered if this was a dream – who didn't dream of being smiled at by a pod of dolphins? But Fliss knew that this was the wild and if they felt they were in danger, the dolphins might become aggressive. Especially if they thought she was going to hurt their baby.

A few of the dolphins suddenly broke away from the pod and sped towards her – their bodies weaving through the water with speed and purpose. Was this an attack? Were they angry with her? Did they think she'd trapped Spinner? Fliss started to swim upwards, and before she knew it she was surrounded.

The dolphins didn't touch her, though. Instead, they swam around her, looking into her mask and nodding, just like Spinner had done. Then they backed away. They weren't trying to scare her off – they were asking her for help! Fliss nodded. She wanted to be a vet. It was her dream to help animals.

But first she needed air.

The dolphins swam with her to the surface, as if they were making sure she wouldn't leave them. They nudged her softly with their noses.

"I'm only human!" she said, gasping for air. "But I'll do my best."

With as much fresh air as her lungs could take, she swam with the pod back to Spinner and inspected the net. It was too tight, too tough. She tore at it with her nails until they ached, but the twine was too thick. Spinner was twisting and turning, but slowly now. He was tiring. And with all the effort she'd used in trying to release the net, she was quickly running out of breath.

She nodded to Spinner. *I'll be back.*

Fliss gulped the air, but as she was

about to go back under, she heard an almighty roar – the growl of engines. Three jet-skis were zooming in her direction. They skimmed across the sea, whisking the surface into a froth of bubbles. In just a few seconds they'd be right above the dolphins and rescuing Spinner would become dangerous. Perhaps even impossible.

"Stop it! Stop it!" Fliss yelled, but her voice couldn't be heard above the noise.

She ducked back underwater to check on Spinner. He was still in the net, rolling from side to side. His family had stopped nudging and pushing. Instead, they hung in the water all around him. It was as if they had lost hope.

And then the jet-skis were there. They made the water crackle and hiss. The dolphins broke out of their sad trance and swam frantically around Spinner again as if it was their last chance to free him. Fliss was finding it harder to stay underwater and the jet-skis were making things worse. She needed to find a way of making them go away.

As Fliss swam up to the surface, she heard Spinner's faint squeal. She turned, clapped her hands and nodded to tell him she'd be back. She just hoped it wouldn't be too late.

On the surface, the jet-skis were so close Fliss could see the drivers' faces. There were two boys and a girl. They whooped with joy as they turned their jet-skis sharply in the water, sending up huge waves and painting the sky with spray. Fliss gasped as she was hit in the face by salty waves. Every time she called out she got a mouthful of water, and each time she lifted an arm to wave for attention she began sinking beneath the waves. But she wasn't worried about herself. She was worried about Spinner.

Fliss found herself at the bottom of the ladder on *Belle* and she climbed aboard.

"Hey!" she shouted. "Stop, please!"

She was sure the jet-skis must have seen her, but they continued to carve up the sea. They were tourists, Fliss decided. A Payocos islander wouldn't dream of coming so close to the precious reef with its delicate coral and wildlife. The jet-skis were dangerously near.

They raced and stopped, again and again. The waves rocked *Belle* from side to side and Fliss was thrown back and forth across the deck. She had to do something quickly – she didn't know how much longer Spinner had left.

Taking the Bait

The jet-skiers had started to race around the boats, rocking them violently. At first, Fliss was frightened *Belle* might capsize. Then she was just plain angry.

The tourists must know how close to the reef they were. It was impossible to ignore the change in sea colour, from deep blue to brilliant turquoise. Fliss wished she was back there, in the safety of the shallow water. But she had to save Spinner. If she didn't … she couldn't bear to think about it.

But first she had to stop the tourists from ruining the rescue.

Fliss staggered into the cabin and gripped on to the boat's wheel to steady herself. She looked at the basic controls. If she could find a phone or radio she might be able to get a signal to someone on Payocos. They could send help right away.

"Come on, come on!" she said to herself, looking around desperately. "There's got to be something here."

But there was no radio. What was she going to do?

"Think, Fliss!" she said. "What would a vet do?"

Animals can't tell humans what the matter is, so vets have to think fast and make decisions using whatever information they have. That's how Fliss saw this situation. She had to make do with what she had. And what she had was a fishing boat with little on board other than a tub of smelly fish bait.

Just then, the girl on the jet-ski zoomed close, unaware of the creatures she was putting in danger. Fliss would have loved to throw that bucket of stinky fish guts all over her!

Aha...

Fliss dragged the bucket to the edge of the boat. She had a plan. And if it worked, she would be back with Spinner very soon.

As the three jet-skis roared nearer, Fliss took a handful of fish bait – old

guts and tails and skin and scales –
and threw it. And then another. And
another. Fliss was only trying to get the
jet-skiers' attention, but the fish bait
landed with a splat on their faces, necks
and shoulders. In horror, they came to a
sudden stop. They stared at her.

"What did you do that for?" the girl asked.

Fliss thought quickly. Use what you know! These people were probably tourists, and Sandy's words came to her... *Tourists are always afraid of sharks.* That's it!

"I'm sorry. I had to get you to stop! I wanted to warn you – there's a whole school of sharks down there. Vicious bull sharks. If you fall off..." Fliss didn't finish the sentence. She thought it was better if the jet-skiers, now covered in shark bait, worked it out for themselves.

"Let's get out of here!" one of the boys shouted.

And they did. They revved their engines and shot back out to sea, away from the reef for good, Fliss hoped.

Now there was no time to lose. Fliss leaped into the water. Immediately, she could see the pod had gone. The annoying jet-skis had scared them away. What about Spinner? She peered around, trying to make out his shape in the deep. But the place where he had been was now a void – an area of nothing.

Then she heard it – a squeal. It sounded so thin and weak, it was as though Spinner had nothing left. Fliss realized he had been washed further out to sea.

"Oh, Spinner!"

Fliss had been so brave. She had conquered the triangle of open sea between the reef, the boats and the place where Spinner had first got tangled. It was just a few swimming strokes to each point. But now he had drifted far out of her comfort zone, and she knew she had to be braver than ever before.

"I'm coming, Spinner!" she said.

Before Fliss could think about being alone in the deep without anything to hold on to, she swam. She swam as fast as she could.

Caught in the Net

It was just Fliss, the deep blue water and, somewhere, a baby dolphin that was in real trouble.

"Spinner, it's me. Where are you?" Fliss shouted into the water. She knew he would recognize her voice. She waited. "Spinner! Talk to me!"

Then, finally, a squeal pierced the silence, followed by another! Fliss swam towards the sound and called for Spinner again. This time, Spinner

answered with a click and a whistle. She
was getting closer. Spinner's replies were
getting louder. But his cries were short
and sharp. He was scared.

"I'm close now," Fliss said, trying to
reassure him. "I'm really close. Hang on
in there!"

Fliss peered down into the blue from
the surface so she could bob up for air
easily. She needed to save her energy
for when she found Spinner. She didn't
know how she would release the baby
dolphin from the net, but she would do
it. She was determined.

"Any moment now, I'll see you. You're
not alone," she murmured.

Squeals came from up ahead and Fliss
could make out a pale shape. She could
see the frayed edges of a large fishing

net, drifting like jellyfish tendrils. Yes! She'd found him! But Spinner wasn't alone.

A dark shape was circling him. At first Fliss thought it was a member of his pod. But as she swam closer, she realized that this wasn't a dolphin shape. It was flatter, leaner. It moved effortlessly through the water. It had stripes, but not like any dolphin she'd seen. Its tail was a different shape too. It cut upright through the water like a boat rudder. It was designed to swish from side to side, not to flick up and down like a dolphin.

By the time Fliss realized what it was, the tiger shark had seen her. It approached slowly and she saw its blank stare pass across her body. It was small, perhaps only a baby, but Fliss was chilled to the bone. She was too terrified even to scream. She was going to be a shark's dinner. This was it – Payocos's first ever shark attack…

But the shark slid by and went back towards Spinner. A dying baby dolphin would be an easier target. Rage bubbled up inside her.

"No you don't!" Fliss screamed, her voice crackling through the water.

She started to swim towards the shark. What was she doing? She was scared of deep water, sharks and drowning. And what could she possibly do? She was slow and unused to the watery world. But something was driving her. She had promised Spinner. What would he think if she retreated now, leaving him with a shark, scared and alone?

As she got closer to Spinner and the shark, the dolphin started nodding frantically and thrashing from side to side. Fliss knew why.

Don't worry about me! I'm staying. The only thing that's going to run away is that shark.

Hoping the young shark was only

being curious, she swam towards it and pushed her hands gently against its rough skin, guiding it away. It didn't mind, but it didn't leave either. She was going to have to be more forceful.

Fliss stretched out her arms and legs to make herself look as big as possible. She pushed the shark's body again. This time it flipped round to face her. Fliss continued to wave her arms and legs, trying to look threatening. Then the shark came too close. Fliss flailed her arms, trying to propel herself backwards. In the flurry, her seashell pendant knocked against the creature's eye. The shark's eyelid automatically slid shut for protection, but it was annoyed. It slithered back towards Spinner.

Scaredy-cat, Fliss thought, although

her heart was beating fast. Then the shark turned and came for her, building up speed as its tail swished from side to side.

Bop it on the nose! Sandy's words popped into her mind.

Fliss got her fists ready. The shark zoomed towards her and she bopped it – bam! bam! – on the nose. And again – bam! bam! The young shark looked stunned.

It turned and snaked off into the deep.

This time, it didn't come back.

Fliss was dizzy and her lungs were screaming for air. She swam up to the surface and breathed in deeply until her head stopped spinning. Then she went down again. This time she would rescue Spinner. The poor dolphin was now tilting to one side, as a single air bubble escaped from his blowhole.

"Spinner!" she shrieked.

Fliss tried to yank the net upwards, but it was too big and awkward. It was no good. Spinner had to be cut free. She needed something sharp. Perhaps there was a knife on the boat? But if she went to look for one, would she get back in time?

It didn't look as though she had a choice. She cradled Spinner's head and stroked his nose. *I'll be as quick as I can*, she thought, hoping that Spinner would understand that she wasn't abandoning him.

Then Spinner began biting at her necklace. *He doesn't want me to go!* she thought.

Fliss pulled the shell from his mouth but Spinner bit at it again. Fliss was worried he would break the beautiful shell. Then she had a memory of a sudden pain in her foot. A sharp cut. A razor edge.

Yes, Spinner, you clever dolphin!

Fliss held the shell steady as Spinner bit down on it with the last of his strength, snapping it in two. Then she used the sharp edge to saw at the net until it started to fray. Spinner twisted to increase the pressure on the thinning strings. One by one they snapped, until finally the remaining net broke away into little pieces. It wouldn't be hurting any more animals now.

Fliss's lungs burned as her oxygen ran out, but she had to hold on … just a little bit longer … for Spinner. He was now motionless and exhausted. He had been without air for ten or fifteen minutes. Too long for a little dolphin. Fliss gritted her teeth and dived underneath him. She dropped the broken shell, placed her palms on Spinner's tummy and pushed upwards, moving him towards the surface.

Sensing freedom, Spinner shot forwards, using his very last drop of energy. He broke through the surface, spat out the old air from his blowhole and breathed again.

Fliss bobbed up beside him, panting and gasping, clutching her chest. It burned with pain. She needed to rest but she was in the middle of nowhere. Her muscles were drained and she was too tired even to tread water. She was sinking back down. She was going to drown… Then Spinner was right by her side.

He tilted his body towards her, brushing his thick dorsal fin against her arm. She took hold of it with both hands and allowed him to tow her towards the reef.

How to Celebrate
with a Dolphin

Fliss dragged herself on to a rock and
sat on the very edge of the reef, between
the light and dark blues of Payocos's
incredible waters. Spinner was saying
thank you with a very special display.
He disappeared into the blue and then
leaped out of the water, spinning in the
air many times before landing with a
splash.

"Bravo, Spinner!" Fliss clapped, as she

counted three full spins. "You're a gold medal gymnast!"

Fliss was exhausted and her arms and legs felt like jelly. But she couldn't have been happier as she sat in paradise, being entertained by Spinner, a baby dolphin that could have died but was now free. It was thanks to her vet's oath – the promise she made to care for animals in danger. She didn't suppose many vets had to fight off sharks doing their job, so she was even a little bit proud of herself.

"What are you doing, Spinner?"

The dolphin was balancing upright on his tail, nodding at her. He disappeared under the water and then surfaced right next to her. He balanced on his tail again and nodded.

"Oh, you want me to come in for a swim?"

Fliss was tired, but would she ever get the chance to see a baby dolphin in the wild again? Or play with one? If she stayed close to the reef she'd be OK, she decided. She could climb up and take a rest when she needed to. She pulled the mask on to her face and leaped over Spinner's head into the water just beyond. Spinner spun with glee and then circled her.

Underwater, Fliss and Spinner met face to face. His dark almond eyes peered into her mask and held eye contact. It was as if the little dolphin was taking time out from his fun to say something. *Thank you.*

You're welcome, Spinner, Fliss thought. *And thank you too.* She felt like the luckiest girl alive.

Spinner then released a huge bubble from his blowhole. It spread out in a perfect circle towards her, as big as a hula-hoop.

Is that for me? Fliss wondered. She swam forwards, using her dolphin-kick to push herself through the bubble ring. "Ta-da!" she burbled in the water.

Spinner opened his mouth and made a
clicking sound. A laugh? Then he blew
another hoop and another – a whole
string of bubble rings – and Fliss swam
through them all. Spinner seemed to
love it. Fliss stopped and nodded. *Your
turn.*

Spinner understood. He swam right
through it, just as she had. Wow! This

was so much fun! Fliss rose to the
surface and danced in the water with
happiness, waving her arms. Spinner
copied, rocking his body from side to
side.

"Let's play follow the leader!" said
Fliss.

She dived down and Spinner followed.
She rolled on to her back. Spinner swam
upside down. She clapped three times.
Spinner clicked three times. Then they
both came up for air, laughing.

Fliss never wanted to bring the game
to an end, but she was very tired now.
She needed to get out of the water and
allow her skin to dry. Her fingertips
were wrinkly as prunes! First, she
beckoned to Spinner and he came to her.

"Spinner, I've had the best time. I

never imagined I'd be friends with a dolphin! But I'm a land animal and I need to rest. I also need to find my way home, and so do you! You're too little to be away from your pod. You need your mother's milk. You should go." Fliss held out her hand and Spinner brushed it with his fin. "High-five, Spinner! We make a great team."

Fliss swam to the reef and climbed on to the rock. The beach in the distance looked inviting. Her tummy rumbled. Some coconut chips and a glass of fruit juice at Izad's shack was exactly what she needed. But Spinner didn't agree. He was still next to the reef, popping out of the water every now and then to look at her.

"No more games now, Spinner. We

both need to get home."

But Spinner wouldn't go and Fliss started to worry. Dolphins lived in pods – they weren't supposed to be alone. Especially not a baby one. She remembered the tiger shark. There would be bigger ones out there…

"You can't hang around here, you have to go and find your family."

Spinner had started somersaulting in the air and tail-walking backwards and forwards to get her attention. Fliss shook her head and crossed her arms, trying to look serious. Spinner didn't understand. He only seemed to understand having fun and playing games.

Fliss had an idea. It was crazy and she was dangerously tired, but she couldn't walk away until she knew he was safe.

"Another game of follow the leader, then," Fliss called. She jumped back into the sea and Spinner circled her with joy – his playmate was back!

Fliss ignored his bubble rings and tail walks and swam out to sea. She tried not to think of sharks and the deep water below her. She kept her mind on her mission – reuniting Spinner with his pod. Spinner followed, nudging her to roll over or play a game, but she had another game in mind. They were two pool lengths out past the reef when Fliss stopped. She trod water to get her breath and then dived under.

What she saw made her heart skip a beat and her head explode with wonder.

Click, Click, Whistle

Fliss had been quietly frightened of what she would see when she went into the deep again. She had feared seeing the smooth sleek shape of a larger sea creature. But this was something else!

As big as a bus, the shark cruised below her. Its skin was dusky grey and covered in white spots, like confetti. A wide mouth gaped as it looked for food, but it wasn't interested in Fliss or Spinner. It only ate plankton and small fish. It was perfectly harmless.

Fliss had always dreamed of seeing a whale shark. She'd seen one on a television programme and envied the camera people who had swum alongside it. This was her chance!

Come on, Spinner! Fliss beckoned.

Fliss and Spinner dolphin-kicked alongside the magnificent beast, avoiding its big mouth. She didn't want to get sucked inside by accident! She took in as much as she could – the colours, the patterns and the texture of its skin – so she would never forget it. If only she could swim with it forever... In fact, how long *had* she been swimming with it?

Fliss surfaced and looked around her. She was a long, long way from the Blue Halo reef now – its bright blue waters visible as just a sliver in the distance. Her heart started to pound. *Stay calm*, she told herself. *Panicking won't do you any good.* It wouldn't help Spinner find his family either. Where *was* he anyway?

"Spinner?" she shouted. "Spinner!"

Oh no... Had he become annoyed

with her for showing the whale shark so much attention? Had he been scared away by something more deadly? Suddenly Fliss felt alone and vulnerable. She was treading very deep water with little energy and no idea of what was below her. Just when she thought she might cry, a little dolphin shot out of the water and arced through the air above her! Fliss held back tears of joy.

"You're like a kid who's had too many sweets!" she scolded. "Playtime is definitely over. It's time to call your family. Ready?"

Fliss dived down and squeaked like a mouse. Spinner copied. She did it for longer. Spinner did it for longer too. Then, after they had both surfaced for more air, Fliss tapped her mask.

Tap-tap-tap. Spinner peered into it, making her laugh. But it wasn't what Fliss was after. She tapped it again and she clicked her tongue. Spinner backed away. He understood and he started to copy her.

Spinner's clicks were so loud, Fliss felt them vibrating through her body. His squeals were so piercing, she had to put her fingers in her ears. But he was doing it! He thought he was playing follow the leader, but in fact he was making his voice heard.

"That's right. Do it again!" Fliss tapped her mask and squeaked like a mouse.

The dolphin was so keen to impress her that he made noises Fliss knew would reach far out to sea. She only hoped that his pod hadn't given up hope and left the area.

"Keep going. We have to keep going." She tapped and squeaked and Spinner did the same, and then … dorsal fins appeared in the distance, slicing through the water. Twenty or thirty of them. A pod of dolphins!

"We did it, Spinner! They've come!" Fliss cried.

Spinner nodded, then placed his fin under her hand. It was as if he knew she needed a rest before the swim back to the reef. "Thank you," Fliss panted, grabbing hold of it tightly. "I just need to catch my breath."

She was confident that the pod would do her no harm. But as they torpedoed through the water towards Spinner, they knocked her sideways and she lost her grip on his fin. They began circling him in celebration, creating a whirlpool, and Fliss felt the water pressure pushing her under. The collision had knocked the breath out of her. She needed air. But the busy dolphins were above and around her and there was no way through.

"Spinner!" Fliss used her last air to shout his name. She had nothing left. She kept her mouth shut tight. Her vision began to blur – it was turning dark as she drifted downwards…

Something soft touched her stomach. Had she reached the seabed at the bottom of the ocean?

The Island

Something rushed at her. It was sudden and fast. Fliss shut her eyes tight to protect them from the blast of water that pushed at her face. She felt around her with one hand. She could feel bodies, and thick dolphin skin. There were dolphins all around her! They were swimming and she was moving alongside them. Then she realized the water wasn't rushing at her, she was rushing through it!

The Island

Within seconds Fliss was at the surface. She was dizzy and gasping for air, and she blinked against the sunlight and seawater in her eyes. She had been saved! She was alive! She was ... *sitting on a dolphin!*

It hadn't been the seabed against her tummy at all. A large dolphin had swum beneath her and scooped her up. She was now sitting on it like a horse. She was riding a dolphin! She had rescued their little calf and they had rescued her!

A tide of relief washed over Fliss and she lay across the dolphin's back.

"Stay here with me, Mr Dolphin," she whispered. "Please don't go back under!"

If he dropped her back in, she'd fall straight to the bottom like a stone. But the dolphin was as sturdy as a boat and he was swimming slowly, still on the surface, towards land.

"Are you taking me back?" Fliss cried with joy. "Oh, you are! Thank you, thank you."

The entire pod flipped and flapped around her as they made their way towards the bright blue water in the distance. For a moment Fliss imagined she was part of this dolphin pod. They smiled at her, nudged her and looked after her. They were like friends. And where was her best friend, Spinner? She couldn't see him. Perhaps he was feeding after such a long time away from his mother. It was hard to see, though, as all of the dolphins wanted to play! They leaped around her, chirping and clicking.

"Woohoo!" Fliss shouted, as they spun and somersaulted over her head. "You're such show-offs!" she called. "But I love you all!"

Something swelled in Fliss's heart. It was a feeling she couldn't describe. It was as if happiness had reached every part of her body, from her head to her toes.

The turquoise band of shallow waters became bigger as they got closer and Fliss felt a jumble of emotions. She needed dry land – she needed to lie down, to walk and feel human again. But it meant saying goodbye to the beautiful spinning dolphins. Tears welled up in her eyes. It wasn't until she brushed them away that she noticed the bright waters didn't belong to the reef at all. During her adventure with the whale shark and the dolphins, she'd gone off course, drifting further out. This was a little island connected to Payocos by a thin strip of sand. Coral Point! The turquoise waters weren't reef, but the shallow sandy edges of the sea.

The dolphins took her as far as they could without stranding themselves on the beach. It had been so long since she stood upright that Fliss's legs buckled as she touched the ground and she fell with a plop backwards into the water. The dolphins cackled.

"I'd like to see you try to walk on land!" she said.

Fliss sat on the beach, watching as her friends played in front of her. She still couldn't see Spinner. She searched the dorsal fins and faces that bobbed above the water. Apart from some of the bigger dolphins, which had scars and scrapes from a life at sea, they all had the same markings, the same sleek bodies and long noses. Still, she knew she'd recognize Spinner in an instant. But he wasn't there. Perhaps the poor little thing was exhausted too.

The dolphins started to move away from the beach. Fliss watched them go, straining to look at every last detail. She wanted to remember it all. Even when they entered the darker waters, she kept her eyes on their shiny backs that dipped in and out of the water, like gentle rolling waves. She waved and shouted "goodbye" long after they had disappeared from sight.

Then she was alone. The beach on Coral Point was beautiful, with soft white sands, swaying palm trees and bright green vegetation. There were banana trees and coconut trees… Fliss's tummy rumbled. She gorged on ripe bananas and she cracked a hole in a coconut with a sharp rock and drank the warm water inside. Then she watched the sun go down, wondering why she was still in paradise. She had saved a dolphin and returned him home. If she had been put here for a reason, that was surely it!

Just then, in the fading light, she saw a baby turtle scuttle past her towards the water. "Hey, little one, where are you going?"

From behind her, hundreds of the little flat-footed creatures were staggering from their sandy nests further up the beach, heading for the ocean. It was an incredible sight.

"Good luck!" called Fliss.

When the last baby turtle had flopped into the sea, Fliss stood up and looked around. The water was turning silvery, the turquoise disappearing with the light.

"I get it!" she exclaimed. "Shells wash up on the beach, but tides return them to the sea. Turtles lay their eggs on land, but the hatchlings always go back to the water. Maybe I'm the same!"

She had come here by being in water, so perhaps that's how she had to return. And now that the dolphins had gone, it was a sign that her time on the white sands of Payocos was up.

Fliss took off her reef slippers and mask and placed them on the beach. She stepped carefully into the water, feeling for sharp shells with her toes. She went

in up to her shoulders and stood still
for a moment, taking a last look at the
tropical island Ella would go nuts for.
Then something knocked against her
leg. Fliss stepped backwards in fright.

It was Spinner!

The little dolphin's face appeared
above the water. Fliss shrieked and held
out her arms.

"Spinner, you've come to say
goodbye!" She cuddled his neck and
stroked his
back. The
dolphin had
something
in its
mouth. "Is
that a gift,
for me?"

Spinner nodded. Fliss took the shell from his mouth. It was a huge, pearly, multi-coloured abalone shell, just like the one she'd lost. Only this one was bigger and brighter and even more beautiful.

When she looked up, the dolphin was gone. "Bye, Spinner. Thanks for everything."

It was time. Fliss looked at the shell in her hands. Should she let go of it? Not this time. She didn't take it from the beach, after all – it was given to her. *A gift from the sea to me*, she smiled, *and it's a good reason to come back to Payocos one day*.

Then she stepped further into the sea and the water closed over her head.

On Dry Land

For a moment, Fliss thought she had
ended up back at the reef. Colourful coral
and shoals of bright fish surrounded her.
But they weren't swaying or swimming
with the underwater currents. They were
perfectly still. Fliss reached out to touch
them to be sure and her fingers met the
swimming pool wall.

She surfaced, held on to the side of the
pool and wiped the water from her eyes.

"You dropped your goggles." Huey

was at her side.

"Thanks, Huey." Fliss blinked.

"They fell to the bottom right in the middle of the pool. I know it can be scary being out of your depth, so I got them for you."

Fliss might have found being out of her depth scary before. But now? She had proved that she could tread water, swim above and below water, dive deep and kick fast. She had proved that she was brave. What would Huey do if he found himself face to face with a tiger shark, she wondered...

"Huey, what would you do if you were swimming in the sea and—"

Mr Luck's whistle shrilled loudly. Fliss would have to find out the answer another time.

"Make your way to the shallow end, please," Mr Luck called. As it was only Fliss and Huey at the deep end, everyone turned to look at them. Fliss tapped Huey on the shoulder.

"Dolphin-kick race?"

"Yeah, all right," he grinned.

With their feet on the back wall, they counted to three and pushed off. Deep down, right on the bottom, they rolled and kicked the whole length of the pool. They surfaced at the shallow end to the sound of cheering.

"Well, there's no question – you two are definitely going to be in the new under-twelves team," Mr Luck said, clapping his hands. "Great control. Fliss, you've come on in leaps and bounds!"

"She's a fast learner," Huey said, high-fiving Fliss.

Everyone started to get out of the water but Mr Luck blew his whistle again.

"Before we finish the lesson, we need some team names. Have you thought of any?"

"How about The Inflatables?" Ella called, still sitting in the donut.

"That makes us sound as if we could be easily popped!" Mr Luck laughed. "Anyone else?"

"The Cannonballs!" Karl shouted.

"That suggests sinking to the bottom... How about something more physical and lively."

"The Spinners," Fliss said. Everyone looked at her. "Like spinner dolphins. They're super-fast but can also do lots of tricks."

"I think we have a winner!" Mr Luck said.

"When does she get the tickets to a tropical island?" Ella said quickly. "I'm her best friend, so I'll be going too, obviously."

Fliss shook her head and laughed at her funny friend.

"The prize is…"

"A submarine!" Kevin shouted.

"I bet it's an extra swimming lesson," Maya groaned.

"If you'll let me finish," Mr Luck tutted. "The prize is something very special. At every swimming gala from now on we'll be collecting money to donate to a charity of our choice. Fliss, would you like to choose the charity?"

Fliss didn't need even a second to think. "A charity that rescues dolphins."

"How about International Dolphin Rescue?" suggested Huey. "I love dolphins," he added.

"Me too," Fliss said. She wondered if one day she'd tell Huey about her experience. But would he ever believe it?

"What's that?" Ella tugged at the hem of Fliss's swimming costume. Tucked inside the leg was a large flat object. Ella yanked it out and held it in the air. "A shell! Where did you get that from?"

Fliss blushed. "The reef down at the deep end," she said. It was pretty much the truth! "It's an abalone shell."

"Mr Luck, Mr Luck, come and see what Fliss has got!"

She handed it to the teacher.

"What a remarkable specimen," said Mr Luck.

"You didn't buy it from a shop, did you?" said Huey, leaning over to look. "I heard you shouldn't buy shells because they're stolen from the sea."

"No, I found it, and one day I'll return it," Fliss said. "I know how important it is to protect our coral reefs."

"Is it a big oyster shell?" Mr Luck said, handing it back. "Where did you get it?"

Where did she get it? What should she say?!

Thanks to cheeky Ella, she didn't have to say anything.

"Mr Luck, it's not an oyster. It's a baloney. Anyone can see that," Ella said, matter-of-fact. "Baloneys are very special."

"I hope you meant *abalone*," Fliss said, giggling.

"What's a baloney then?"

"A salami sausage."

Ella shrieked and covered her mouth. Then she ran off to tell everyone else her hilarious mistake as they walked to the changing rooms.

Fliss was the last to go. She stood by the pool and looked down at the coral reef mural. She already missed the beautiful sea plants and pretty fish. She even missed the bigger creatures in the deep blue beyond. But most of all she missed the playful little dolphin.

"I'll think about you every day," she said under her breath.

She began to walk away when there was a plopping sound in the pool. She turned back quickly. A large silvery bubble ring rose up through the water from the bottom of the pool and burst on the surface, splashing Fliss.

"Ha ha, Spinner. Very funny. And that reminds me, it's time I paid Ella back!"

Fliss scooped up some water and headed towards the changing rooms to splash Ella, feeling as playful as Spinner, and wearing a smile just as cheeky.

Rachel Delahaye was born in Australia but has
lived in the UK since she was six years old. She
studied linguistics and worked as a magazine writer
and editor before becoming a children's author. She
loves words and animals; when she can combine the
two, she is very happy indeed! At home, Rachel loves
to read, write and watch wildlife documentaries.
Outside, she loves to go walking in woodland.
She also follows news about animal rights and the
environment and hopes that one day the world will
be a better home for all species, not just humans!

Rachel has two lively children and a dog called
Rocket, and lives in the beautiful city of Bath.